Literature written for young adults...

by young adults.

Allow yourself to be surprised.

Reflecting Our Greatness

Young Writers Anthology

Kelsey Beach
Kelly Piggott
Robert Feldman
Katherine Stevenson
Editors

Derek Koehl
Senior Editor

VERBALEYZE
Press

Atlanta

All the selections are the original work of the authors as cited in the Permissions section.
Edited by Derek Koehl
Cover photo © 2005 Dirk Beyer
ISBN: 978-0-9910209-4-2

VerbalEyze Press books are available at special discounts for bulk purchases in the United States by corporations, institutions and other organizations.

For information, address VerbalEyze Press, 59 Thayer Ave SE, Atlanta, Georgia 30315.

VerbalEyze does not participate, endorse, or have any authority or responsibility concerning private correspondence between our authors and the public. All mail addressed to authors are forwarded, but the publisher cannot, unless specifically instructed by the author, give out an address or phone number.

VerbalEyze Press
A division of VerbalEyze, Inc.
www.verbaleyze.org

Table of Contents

Michael Sweat

Megan Diekhoff

Janay Walker

Eliza Sanders

Critical Reading Questions and Writing Exercises

Reflecting Our Greatness

Foreword

The *Young Writers Anthology* series is a result of the vision that took shape four years ago. That vision—to foster, promote and support the development and professional growth of emerging young writers—is the guiding principle for everything we do at the VerbalEyze Writers Cooperative and through VerbalEyze Press. The *Young Writers Anthology* series embodies two components of the VerbalEyze mission: one, to engage young people in and with creative writing and two, to provide talented young writers the opportunity to become published authors and learn the business aspects of being a professional writer.

Technology is transforming more than the mechanics of book publishing; we believe it enables a transformation of the very fabric of the publishing industry. VerbalEyze is working to bring the advantages of a new publishing approach to today's generation of young writers.

In addition to the craft of writing, we teach young people the business of writing and a revolutionary framework for writing and publishing that is fully cooperative. With the *Young Writers Anthology* series and our innovative royalties model, we are enabling young writers to say, "I am my scholarship!"

We thank you for the support you have shown these young writers through the purchase of this anthology. *Reflecting Our Greatness* brings you some of the most outstanding poetry and short stories by young writers whose middle school and high school ages stand in contrast to the power of their words and the depth of their vision into the human condition.

Allow yourself to be surprised. We did.

The Editors

Note to Educators

"Before one can think critically, one must be able to think creatively."

Fellow educator,

Whether you are a public or private school teacher, a home school teacher, or youth worker, our goals are the same: to engage the creative capacity latent in all our children and teach them to harness that capacity to bring about change in their own lives and in the world around them. *Reflecting Our Greatness,* the latest edition of the *Young Writers Anthology* is aligned with these objectives in two ways.

First and foremost, this anthology is literature written by young people. Engagement with the creative qualities of literature is instrumental to the process of awakening creativity in students. I believe this engagement is strengthened by the perception of shared experiences and perspectives that occurs when a reader identifies with a writer.

Second, the editorial team at VerbalEyze Press contains several members who are also professional educators. For each selection in the anthology we have provided a critical reading question and a writing prompt, all aligned with the Common Core State Standards. The critical reading questions help focus students on core thematic and analytical aspects of the selections. The writing prompts variously challenge students to write in explanatory, analytic and creative modes as they respond to or reflect on central ideas and concepts within each selection.

We have invested our energies into making the *Young Writers Anthology* series a reality for one simple reason: we believe in young writers and young people. We are encouraged that you share that belief.

Derek Koehl, M.Ed.

Caisa Doyle

Not Alone

The yellow moon woke me early that morning, its steady, glowing beams shining brightly into my eyes. I'd forgotten to close the gray curtains before retiring to bed. As my eyes wandered around the room, steely shadows danced on the walls–harmless shadows of course, but shadows all the same. The fog that collected on my windowpane did not help to decrease the haunting tone that concealed the innocuous reality of the walls that surrounded me. Outside, dogs barked as if attempting to warn me of a danger that was not there and the rumbling of the cars, whose engines sputtered and choked as they moved, rushed by but did nothing to comfort me as I rose up from where I lay and pulled back the pale polyester bed sheets that worked as a shield against the monsters that hid in the darkness. Nearly running to the light switch that resided by the door, my heart raced in anxiety, in the light that I had believed to be my refuge, I realized with terror that I was not as alone as I had thought.

Reflections

He screams at me, but I'm not listening. Just because his words are loud does not make them real. I frown, my eyes falling and latching onto the hand mirror that perches tediously on the edge of the desk to my left. Framed in tarnished silver, the mirror bears a name of someone I never knew. They died long before the mirror came into my hands, but I feel as familiar with them as if they stand in the room at this very moment.

"Are you even listening to me?" he asks, taking a furious step towards me. My attention snaps to him for a single second before flickering back to the mirror. He moves closer, still, and I retreat. He says something about me always being *like this*. I don't care.

Words tumble from his lips without a pause. They pierce my chest, like I've gotten caught in a storm armed with daggers instead of raindrops. He isn't thinking about how this hurts me. This is how he really feels about it, how he really feels about me.

I haven't spoken this whole time. Not a single word. I seem to be at a loss while he aims each sentence at me to make me fall, taking me down with as much pain as possible. It's working.

I move away from him again, my hip hitting the side of the table and knocking the mirror to the floor. We both watch it slip from its place on the table, and its ear-splitting crash bringing us to a standstill. Neither one of us looks away from the glass on the floor. One piece captures my teary face and another has caught his; it looks just as broken as the glass that portrays it. The other pieces show images around the room: gray bed sheets, blue curtains, my bare legs. Everything around us shattered.

His eyes catch mine, and he opens his mouth to apologize.

"Get out," I mutter. He prepares to protest, but, for some reason, doesn't.

He leaves the apartment quietly.

The clock is blaring 1 a.m. when he gets home, so drunk that he can barely stand. We get into bed and fall asleep together like old lovers, the broken glass screaming on the floor.

Stormy

The rain pours down so heavily that I can't see through it. Everything has lost its color in the storm. Clouds are lower than usual; I wish that they were not within reach. Lightning strikes the water and waves cower away from it. I can relate.

The tree to my left is almost dead, but not much farther off to my right is one that flourishes with life. Wind blows in my face and I feel my soul begging to let it push us away from this painful place. But the white sand on the beach holds my feet to the ground like glue. It doesn't want me to leave. I can feel the shadows become heavier around me and my own chest seems to get weighed down by the darkness.

But then it stops. Everything stops. My heart stops. Or maybe it starts beating. I am unsure. But something changes around me and all I see is water dripping from branches and wet leaves on the ground and the stillness of the lake. The clouds still hang but they are empty now, they have run out of things to cry about. I wish I were like the clouds.

Instructions for Anxiety Attacks

Don't think about the reasons that make the world feel like it's ending or the stuff that put that panicky feeling that you just can't shake into your bones. For now, we should understand the inevitability of this anxiety attack and how we ought to go about having it. Step one: knot your stomach carefully, be sure that to bind your intestines as securely as possible- they will be your tether you to the freezing tiles of the empty kitchen you've found yourself in. Next, coil your chest so taught that you feel like an elephant has made your breast its new resting place. Do not make the mistake of choosing a lighter animal; this will only make things worse. By now, one's eyes should be watering with a concoction consisting mainly of fear and basic nausea.

Now that you are off to a good start, let's take a moment to examine the thoughts rampaging around your head. For the average sufferer, something simple is more than enough. However, make sure that you always have a large selection of ideas and what if's on-hand to avoid getting bored with the concept of impending doom.

Don't forget the essentials: wrench a few sobs or sob-like gasps from your throat- yes, I know it feels like someone's standing on it, that's okay. If you can't think straight, you're right on track. Are you dizzy? Perfect. If you feel like you'll die if someone touches you, you're doing things right. The final step is, of course, to add your own personal touch. Throw in some weak knees or make sure there's no way you can get enough air into your lungs to live through this. This should continue for an average of 10 minutes, but do not hesitate to proceed in waves of grief for the following two hours. If, following this event, every part of your body is tired and sore, then you have succeeded in having the ideal anxiety attack.

The Doorman

His reputation lives within the door of The Osborne. The apartment building located at 205 West 57th Street is his main source of income. He holds the door for people for ten hours a day.

He has no friends, no family, his only companionship is the mahogany frame and polished glass. Everyone who knows Ian knows him as the doorman for the expensive residency.

For hours, he stands there, smiling at passersby and opening the door for those floating in our out of the building with the occasional nod of thanks.

The door stands tall and weighs more than it should. This is something the man and the door have in common. The man just reaches six feet five inches and weighs a little too much due to the ready-made meals that crowd his refrigerator.

He's worked here for thirty years, starting when he was twenty-four and new to the city. They kept him despite his graying hair and wrinkling skin, just as they had kept the door.

He wasn't always known for the door. Once he had a best friend and a mother and a father. He even had a little sister and 'pals' to get a beer with on Wednesday nights. But they left long ago, his creaking personality driving them away.

The door whines as he pulls it open and lets people out. He understands.

 **Caisa Doyle** wrote her first novel at age fourteen. She has always been a lover of books due to her dad reading such works as *The Hobbit*, *Stuart Little*, *Charlotte's Web*, and *Harry Potter* to her when she was just five. Caisa is a senior in high school and hopes to major in creative writing when she goes to college. She lives in Houston with her parents and younger sister, Zoë, and five cats.

To prevent the "Hermione Syndrome", we will tell you now that the "Cai" name is pronounced like Cairo, Egypt. She spends her time writing short stories and poetry as well as reading novels by the truckload. She hopes to one day be the author of a full length young adult novel as well as a collection of short stories.

Jordon Rucker

Mirror

You're my reflection
Baby you must be an angel
'Cause when the spotlight
Hit you just right
You are a glistening star
You know exactly who you are
I glimpse in the mirror
To make sure you're still there.
But lies distort you
You as my reflection turns around
I see your heart in broken pieces
Because your world has fallen apart
Tears fall as you look down
Baby please don't look down

Suffer in Silence

How dare you stand there
                              Watching me
Crying and trying to fit in
Running away from the grip of my captor
Inside a cold dark society
Fear is my reality
That's why I am mentally running

I sit here inside of this crypt
Tied by my waist
My lips silenced by force
I struggle trying to get out of this rope
Pull my sweaty palms from this grip
Walk strongly out that door
       But I hear the floor creak
             My captor stands behind me
                   I tumble to the floor

                        Dragged back by my legs

He forces me into a chair
He hits me angry
It's easier if I simply suffer in silence

Please Answer

Ring Ring
Ring Ring
    Call forwarded to an automatic voicemail system
Please leave a message for...
    Typical Old Pops
    Guess he's getting chased by the cops again
    I wonder what he did this time
    Steal a car?
    Drunk while driving?
    Shot someone?
And it's sad that I looked up to this dude
He doesn't even have the time to answer a call from his son
Are your smokes and drinks more important than your blood?
    Please answer, Dad
    Because I want you to hear my wrath
    Yes I'm mad
    I believed every lie that came out of your mouth
Saying you loved me
That you cared, but if you did
You wouldn't be dead to me
    Ring Ring
    Ring Ring
    Please leave your message for
    3-323-232-8323

Back When

Counting how many invisible tears will fall before I care, there goes

1

How dare you cut into my chest and steal an

2

Artificial fragment of desperate love

3...4

It's just because I felt sorry for your

5

Disappointment that nobody wants

6

Edit—forget it
No forget you
Remember when you said you wanna

7

I'll never do this again
You're just a screw
Hiccup ...   8

Time's up
You're love struck

9

You're lucky
Chose you but girl you're nothing new

10

Jordon Rucker

Mad Hatter

I tip my hat
just to where she can see my vibrant red cheeks

She's the only one that honestly knows
 the truth
because she was the one who jumped off her roof and skyrocketed
    down this hole
 her insecurities blush in her pale cheeks
 her name is Alice
It rings a bell
She nervously runs down streets

'Til her blood doesn't circulate

A small tear released from her eye lids
The world's in slow motion

Darkness appears behind her

Hands of desire yanking her to doom
as I throw tea pots and cups to get to her safety
I run across the long white table

While Alice
 is dragged into a pit
Tick Tock

Reflecting Our Greatness

Time is running out
 She drifts away farther… farther

My hat
     Flips toward the ground
My orange and green hair falls over my face

swinging back and forth
I crouch in front of her chair

I flip my hair over slowly
Alice… Chair has collapsed on the ground
Alice… Is gone

Jordon Rucker started writing in the fourth grade. His first work? A poem for Valentine's Day.

He is now writing and performing as a member of the Ya Heard? Arts Collective. Not only does he have a talent for poetry, but he is also an actor, singer, and dancer. His passion for the arts has him setting his sights on one day attending Julliard. He looks up to icons like Michael Jackson and Maya Angelou for their ability to beautifully showcase their talents and aspires to one day be like them.

Lauren Boisvert

The Last Words of this Poem are a Lie

My body is a propaganda poster and
my womb has a Jewish family in the attic.
I bleed red and terrible and red
and I am declared a national threat.
I am a grey stain on an old mattress.
I am a war hospital pitched at the front lines.
I am an army nurse, Florence Nightingale
in overalls and lipstick.

You make so much noise about sailing
the seas but when given a boat you turn away,
suddenly happy with dry land. I am the boat
left at the dock like a poor bride at the altar.
"Virgin Mary" is painted in terrible red
across my sea-worthy ass, and you leave me
floating under the oncoming storm.

You are a thorn in my little lion paw.
You cause me great pain and yet
I long for suffering. It's not one of my
better qualities but it makes me feel alive.

My body is a torn up old classified
and the Jewish family has been discovered.

Reflecting Our Greatness

I weep for the young girl but I think her book
will be a big hit. I am a rhapsody in red death.
Every month I kill a child. This is the way
it has to be. Every month I kill a ballerina,
an engineer, a president. They are not born
and they belong to no one, because you
do not belong to me anymore.

You are a ghost in my house and I am
the exorcism that gets you out.

My body is an empress of the northern lands
and my womb is barren and blackened by fire.
I sharpen my sword on your broken bones
and the steel gleams like so many teeth.
You put your fingers under my chin
so I cut them off and they bleed red and terrible
and are declared a national threat.
You feel you've been cheated but I don't care anymore.

I have never cared.

My body is a windowpane and you look idly
through me to gaze at your one and only
on the other side. Her body is a rock
and you crash against her like white caps.
I don't care anymore. I have never cared.

I have never cared.

I have never cared.

Lauren Boisvert

Twelve Years of Holly Trees

*"Love is like the wild rose-briar, friendship like the holly-tree –
the holly is dark when the rose-briar blooms, but which will
bloom most constantly?"*

– Emily Brontë

If friendship is like the holly tree then let ours
be a Christmas wreath on the front door of a big house,
somewhere up North where the snows
blanket the lawns and the wind whips the dead

branches of trees, but inside there is yellow light
and warmth and love like something tangible in
the air. Can you feel it, our friendship, climbing
the front stoop and ringing the bell, dressed warmly

in the scarf I made for you, my pom-pom hat, our
jackets and gloves, and breath clouding the air letting
us know that we're alive, here, now, holly branch
wreath on the front door of a big house, and I see

our friendship in a beautiful string of lights, in the
gooey warmth of an apple pie, in a fireplace raging
in the dead of winter. Inside our friendship like inside
a house there are decorative bundles of twigs and the smells

of baking, the sound of laughter and the clinking of glasses.
Hearts all around my feet and I pick one up and pin it
to your jacket, pin one on mine, and our friendship rejoices
in the little things, a photograph, a whisper into a shell
thrown in the ocean, a poem written and sent in the mail.

Corporate Cannibals Churn Out Ghosts

The watch on your wrist tick tick ticks
away hours and days and weeks
and you're no stronger than you were
when you started. Carrier pigeons take prayers
to the heavens and you wish you could go with them.

The scene changes and you're in a slaughterhouse,
the stench of blood tangible in the air
and when you raise your fingers to touch
they come away wet with it. So it goes
and there's a lamb that won't stop watching you,
eyes beady and black like buttons so you trip
forward and out

into a meadow of poppies fat and red like a blood moon.
A breeze cuts through the heat of daylight and your lover
swings by his neck from a willow tree.

You blink and your eyes are blurry and wet with tears;
it's an unfamiliar sensation to cry for someone.
You can't recall another time you've done it.

The watch on your wrist tick tick ticks
away a year and your heart has hardened
into a peach pit. You let them manhandle you

ɔm your bed, let them shave your head and
ip you of your clothes, let them carve you up
t you but you make them sick with bloody ulcers
d the ghost of your lover laughs sweetly
the shadowy corner of the room.

u devour him with kisses and he laughs like a wind chime
ainst your dark hair grown back in death.
e is a beautiful anomaly in your arms
d your eyes are wet with joy.

Bastard Children

There is a golden quality to the first born;
She is sacred and special and full of promise,
a star with hair like spun gold. She shines ethereal
in the cold damp of a stone house. Her name is
the scent of roses spelled in five letters.

Middle born is a goddess-like accident,
her heart a rocky mountain pass, crooked smile
like craggy cliffs. Her voice is the rustling of leaves
and she is wild as kudzu climbing the walls.
Her name is the six letter sound of antlers
against tree bark.

The last born is precious silver, diamonds, rubies,
a circlet of jewels on a high proud forehead.
She is the blushing portrait of a renaissance girl,
the gently folded hands of a sculpted marble child.
Her four letter name is the blur of impressionism,
Claude Monet's brushstrokes.

The triumvirate sits together in that stone house,
hands clasped in a triangle over a scarred wood table.
They light white pillar candles with a snap of fingers
like breaking twigs, turn their faces to each other
in silent reverence, and pray for their family secret.

 **Lauren Boisvert** is a junior at University of Central Florida studying creative writing. She has had poems previously published in *Mochila Review*, and will be published on *YARN* and in *The Broken Plate* in Spring 2015. Her mom is very proud of her. One time she walked really close to David Sedaris while he was signing books, but he didn't see her; this is her favorite story to tell to strangers. Her personal aesthetic is "cool witch."

Zyan Wynn

Fears

Fear of spiders
Fear of the time
Fear of change
Fear of life
Fear of being different
Fear of being the same
Fear of telling someone
   Basketball is lame
Fear of cars
Fear of wars
Fear of death
Fear of me
At my best
Fear of love
Fear of sex
Fear of the truth
Fear of causing death
Fear of being love
Fear of the sea
Fear of planes

Reflecting Our Greatness

Fear of bees
Fear of chains
Fear of being held down
Fear of happiness
Fear of God
Fear of the devil's kiss
I keep running
Away from Fears
But none are
Chasing me

My biggest fear
Is me

Treasure

Once Upon A Time
I had life
I was me
I was the one
Ivory Silk Dress
Glass Slipper
5 Carat Ring
I had a life
I was me
I was the one
Christmas Morning
Home Filled
Giggles
Glee

I had a life
I was me
I was the one
When the thunder boomed
Kids leaped into
Warmth of my bed
Smiles
Brighter than the Moon
Perfect
Until the day
Thunder cracked

Wind smacked
Husband back
Told me
He got sacked
I was taken aback
Mercedes Benz gone
IPhone 5s sold
Suddenly
Reality brought me back
I was dethroned
Stuff
I had to get it back
Left that day
Big City Guy
New York City
Flight Time: 9:05

Christmas Eve
St. Mary's Church
No family
No husband
No love
A callous C.E.O
I am Eve
Deceived
By Greed
Masked as Need

                                        But once

I was his treasure
He loved me for me

Redefined

I was born a lie
A child born
To a show girl
And some rich white guy
XS Nightclub
Started good
Drinks raised up
Their mind swayed

Raised in an alley
Walls lined
With junk
On Bricks
Cracks inflict
Knees ripped
By holes in cement
This life
Forced to abide
To live as a lie

Woken by a drive by
Walk outside
No emotion
Just another
Dead guy
Flickers of morning light

As shadows of death
Drift by

Book bag
Ready to go
To class
Education
A Ploy
For dough

Head in
See boy against lockers
Wounded flesh
Blackened eyes
Tears of misery
For being
Gay
They say

Bullies surround me
Say
John Doe is here
Run down clothes
Banged up nose
Rotten
Mom's a …
Wait, he already knows

Pondering
Is my life a lie?
Born and raised
As a shadow
Avoiding the light
At school
Where I mask
Grief and fright
My Life
My Worth
Proves
That truth
Is redefined
Over time

Born to Die

The painful silence
broken by a scream
Lifeblood pouring
racking sobs rising
A smug look on the murderer's face,
Tells the whole truth
Tells the whole story

> The truth of

Another black man
Shot down
The sound of the gun

> Registers

The old news story
Black Male Found Dead

> Just another

Lesson learned here
Black Men
We were born to die

Zyan Wynn is a 13-year-old male. His interest in poems stems from his love of expression whether that is through his passionate speeches or emotional poems. He poems are based around political and civil topics as that is where most of his passion comes from.

He was introduced to poetry by his language arts teacher, Mrs. Susan Barnes. At first, Zyan thought of poetry as a expression for people who are too scared to speak. but he came to realize that it is for the people who are strong enough to speak and tell the world their story.

Zyan was born and raised in Atlanta where he currently resides with his loving mother.

Michael Sweat

Blue's Clues

Remember
The dog
Blue
Who
Could follow a clue
I do
Cuz I just made a bang
Where brains flew
And one clue
Is between me
And you
The cop
So I hope that dog
Doesn't know
That we have one
With a blog
Or else he'll find me
And I'll be out like
1
   2
      3...

Leave

Wasted

Can't see
Can't move
Can't feel
Can brood
I forget who
To blame
All I know
Is "It's cool."
That and
CHUG! Chug! chug. chug…
Whoohoo!?!
Yeah right
Not without
A fight
You stupid?
'Fraid so
Oh, well
Too late
Bye bye
John Doe

Banished

I have been cast

Out

An honorary

Outcast

But have decided

Not

To dwell on the

Past

Now is just

Then

When?

Just now will be

Then

So now it's just them

For I am the mastermind

Who is behind the

Phenomenon

Of time

I have become

Me

Because time is

Money

Wait, huh?

Lost in time

Life

Mindless Me

Lumosity

Fortuity

Stupidity

What do these words mean?

　　IDK why you askin' me

'Cuz I swear I'd lose my head if it weren't attached to me

I see a no loitering sign so all I do is lean

Lumosity

Fortuity

Stupidity

What do these words mean?

　　IDK, but I guess they're all that I'm cracked up to be…

Go

Live

Michael Sweat

The World

Disgustingness
And
Disgustingness
Just makes more
Disgustingness
But
Discussing this
Disgustingness
Makes us all
Disgusting less

Free

Michael has always been a story teller; even before he could write! He can't wait to put his dreams down in the written word. He was inspired by rapper Eminem when he heard the song, "The Real Slim Shady." Just like Shady, Michael wants to be one of the greats. He aspires to be a technological entrepreneur while writing novels and poems in his free time.

He lives with his mom, step-dad, brother, and two loyal pups in Atlanta, Georgia, learning all the while, to become a man.

Megan Diekhoff

Tea With my Town

I took a seat for tea with my town.
I was visiting because it had been
a while since I'd said hello
to the ladies always sitting
in the coffee shop on
bleak Sunday afternoons.
Visiting, because somehow
I feared that too many new
crevices would creep into
the sidewalk without my presence.
The ladies shuffled into the door,
each with one hand holding a purse,
one hand clutching a
newspaper or knitting needles or
a cane or someone else's hand.
When they took their seats,
I silently gave a nod and waved.
I drank tea because coffee
was the only other beverage offered
and water seemed insufficient.

Reflecting Our Greatness

Tea, because the last time
I tried a sip of it
I drank from a plastic
Scooby-Doo cup with a bendy straw.
This time I drank from
a chipped glass,
claimed to be antique
but what I felt was the result of
reckless dishwashing and contempt.
After the contents of the glass
had diminished, out of sight,
my town sat—straight, poised,
arms crossed, impatient legs, head tilted
to one side begging me to lean
back into my past, but I licked my lips,
debating between a refill and a
search elsewhere to quench my thirst.

Megan Diekhoff

Antimony's Prayer

I've forgotten I'm brittle and broken
I've forgotten my luster is gone,
pushed away what's too heavy to carry
made room in my heart for a song
Bright sunlight beams all around me
the flowers revive from their snooze,
how funny, the world comes to meet you
if you're willing to let yourself move

The Instant After

I'd focus on anything in the
backdrop of your photo
as long as it wasn't you.
I fixated on the green and blue
children's tables,
all of which demanded attention,
as did the petite and messy
hands that rested on top of them.
Each of these hands was busy;
one flipped the pages of a
picture book
and kept turning back to the
second page because that one
had a duck on it
and ducks were his favorite.
Another set of little fingers
pointed to every word of her book
as she carefully pronounced
each syllable aloud because
her parents told her that she
should try harder at reading.
Hanging from the ivory ceiling
was a balloon that lacked
helium but not motivation,
because every inch of that balloon
was covered with a paper-maché

exoskeleton,
determined to become independent
and separated from the rest.
I tried to stare at the bookshelf
behind you but my eyes
got frustrated with ignoring
your presence in the foreground.
A little boy tapped your shoulder
and shoved into your hands
The Little Engine that Could
from which you called words to life.
Yours was the kind of voice
I could fall asleep to once
but now no longer, so
I crowded that sharp picture
into the depth of my memories
and the instant after
I reached into my satchel,
pulling from it a disposable camera
which had been tossed
alongside the sidewalk of a
nearby convenience store.
It still had a few photos left to take,
so I paused to take a snapshot of
the road ahead of me,
and walked onward,
eager to process the film.

Unravel

The lights are only half on,
the quiet chaos of soft whispers
mingles with the echoes of the pianoforte
as I lean my head against a cabinet
where copies of worn sheet music are stored
I am looking at the way the pianist's hair sets just so
while I fiddle with my own hair,
picturing events of the past,
playing them over and over in my mind,
arpeggios repeating
a familiar melody
In a far corner, a couple is sitting
brushed fingertips against smooth cheeks,
smiling at the empowerment of music and
carpets that jump to life—
suddenly I am in a trance,
finding each differently colored thread,
picking at it,
will it unravel?

Haste

Haste is an eroding characteristic.
She was barely here long enough
to unpack her luggage
before she had already begun
yearning for the road.
She was born knowing how to
cram her life into a carry-on,
how to tip the bellhop without
making eye-contact so she wouldn't
feel compelled to stay.
She grew troubled at the
lack of curtains in her hotel room
and found little consolation in
hiding underneath the sheets.
Her feet ached from running,
but her heart ached from standing still.
And she feared that if she
stayed in one place too long,
the rain would wash her
sedimentary soul away.

The Day My Trampoline Died

The day I stopped fearing love
was the day my trampoline died.
Its brittle grey fibers pulled—almost pushed—
away from each other like a young boy
forced by his mother to
give his sister a hug but who
retracts his arms immediately after the family photo.
I collapsed beside the rift in the seams and
seven years of childhood spilled onto the ground below—
a ground where an army of weeds congregated,
despite the shade and lack of space.
My fingers plucked the faded and lifeless strings like
those of a guitar without tune
but I desperately needed a melody.
The night you sang me a lullaby
was the night I tried to make all my childhood dreams
live again.
I cut out fragments of the resilient trampoline floor
and tucked them into my heart
so the next time I wear it on my sleeve
people will know that I am fully capable of falling in love
and then jumping back up to my feet.
I draped strips of disintegrating net around my shoulders
like a shawl with holes and I watched the sunlight
smile down at the frayed black mess which had too

many seasons of ice-and-thaw-ice-and-thaw
and I remember the evening in which I learned that
frozen souls do thaw,
if only we provide our minds with the sympathy of
hot cocoa and rub our hands together with the
intention to serve in the morning,
the intention of running in circles but
always going somewhere
new

**Megan Diekhoff** is a senior at Southridge High School in Huntingburg, Indiana. She enjoys a variety of activities, one of which is participating in the school's creative writing club. Megan is a member of several academic clubs, tennis, and the annual school musical. She also plays snare drum in the marching band.

During the summer, Megan interns at a local company and helps take orders at her family's ice cream shop (the Windmill Chill) located in Holland, Indiana. She plans to study multilingual speech-language pathology next year in college, and will continue writing as a hobby.

Janay Walker

Don't Judge Me

It happens every time
You get the backstory
But don't even stay
To hear my side
All you wanna hear
Are the lies
That come out
Of other people's mouths
But none of the truth
You could easily get
By asking
But that's too much
Isn't it
Just doesn't fit
With the people
You hang with
So two-faced
'Cause I have to listen
To your point of view
But when it comes to me

Reflecting Our Greatness

That doesn't matter to you
I'm so sick and tired
Of being called the liar
When all that I desire
Is for you to listen to me
Is that too much?
It's such a tragedy
The way we're ending
'Cause you couldn't
do one thing

Don't judge me

Father

Were you nervous?
Were you scared?
I know you were never there
A distant reality
You didn't want another kid
But you realized
Actions have repercussions
All these years
With no memories
No piggy back rides
No build-a-bears
Not even a hug
Not one laugh
With my dear ol' man
Who wasn't there to pick me up
At my first breath
At the beginning of my life
All I knew
You were somewhere
You ran away
But it's time for you to face me
It's time for us to meet
Questions asked
Some dead space
Like
Why didn't you come and see me

Reflecting Our Greatness

Some dead space
A cowardly move
To never see your only daughter
Sure you may be my father
But my daddy isn't you

Daughter

I used to follow the rules
No trouble in school
Did everything anyone asked me to
Always did what I had to do
Until I realized
I have my own voice
And choices
That I have the right to question
Whether this is who I want to be
Always thinking
Steady shrinking
When it comes to stepping up
But then I realized
All my life I already had
I grew up without my biological father
But I always had my dad
Who taught me
To love myself
More than anyone else
I've grown up to realize
That I'm a daughter
Of a selfless beauty
And a man
Who couldn't care any less about me
I've lived in people's shadows
All my life

Reflecting Our Greatness

But now I'm stepping up
And becoming the young woman
I'm meant to be

Janay Walker

What If?

Life is just a game
We're here
Relying on the players
Behind the controllers
Figments of their imaginations
Everything we think matters
Stored in a memory card
Designed for entertainment
So it doesn't matter whether we have hearts or not
What if
No one really dies
Just resurrected by starting a new game
What if words aren't what they mean
And are opposite
Of what they seem
What if heaven was hell and hell was heaven
Do all good deeds
Result in punishment
And all bad deeds
Become achievements
I don't know the answers
But it makes sense
What if the answers are hidden
And there's a secret code to get to them
And there are some people
Who actually know

This vital information
Or is it too far-fetched
To ask what if

Misfit

I am fake on a regular basis
Despite being irritated
The girl who'd put up a fight
If you crossed the line
Whose attitude shows most of the time
But doesn't like taking it out on other people
It just happens
The girl who only loves her close friends and family
Because trust
Which I thought was a must
Was lost
When you left me in the dust
I try time and time again
To be helpful and
Be friendly
But it steady bites me in the butt
No matter what I say or do
I end up disappointing people too
In the mirror I see
Potential hiding
I am
Scared to be seen
'Cause showing it
Means to get bullied
So I stop being the real me

And started talking
To save myself
From revealing
My true identity—
a misfit

Janay Walker became interested in poetry in the fifth grade after going to a school poetry block party. She wrote her first poem as a homework assignment for her fifth grade Language Arts teacher. Some of her close friends asked to hear her poems and told her to start writing as a hobby instead of just doing it when she is bored or has nothing else to do.

She is inspired by Shel Silverstein after reading his poetry book *Where The Sidewalk Ends*. She started writing poems, not goofy hysterical poems, but more problem poetry. She hopes to one day become awell-known poet worldwide.

Eliza Sanders

Rebirth

The soft light filtered in through the crevices between the boulders, showcasing a swirling colony of minute dust particles. The cracked gray stone was cool to the touch, and the surrounding rocks completed the make-shift shelter. This was home, Ember's home.

Crisp foliage crunched beneath her bare feet as she crept into the heart of Dead Forest. Massive trees glared down at her, but she was not afraid. After all, these woods did not breathe, did not live. Her long, platinum blonde hair snagged on a branch, and Ember bit her lip in pain. Deftly, her slender fingers brushed dead-dried leaves aside until she found what she was looking for. The silver teeth of a trap glared up at her, and she sighed in defeat. There would be no breakfast today. Ember felt the hot tears of bitter disappointment begin to run down her face. *No*, she told herself. She never cried, and she would not start now.

"Ember!" the harsh tones of her mother reached her ears. That stupid woman. How she resented her mother. Ever since Pangaea attacked, nothing had been the same. Ember could not help but mentally relive the past four months. The memories were still fresh in her heart.

The first warning shot had rang through the crisp morning, shattering whatever peace there had been. In seconds the city was alive with able-bodied people scrambling for their guns, rushing to the coast to defend us. What we didn't know was that every city, every state in America, was experiencing the same panic and fear. We were under attack, and nothing could've prepared us for it.

Soon, this country was a barren wasteland. Millions died fighting, and even more as prisoners at the hands of Pangaean soldiers. My brother, Sal, and my father were both captured. The soldiers who took them destroyed my home, taking any food we had with them while my mother stood by, silent. I lashed out, trying to save my family, but only got a harsh beating from the soldiers and later my mother.

They were merciless. The bodies of dead babies and children were piled on top of each other and burned. The scent of death lingered on every rotten blade of grass, every blackened tree stump. The smoke covered the sun for days, not a trace of our former lives remained.

Ember was wrenched from her memories as another one of her mother's screams for her shattered the air. She sighed and tilted her head back, closing her eyes. In her mind, this Earth had only just begun. The terror and bloodshed that stained the past was only a preliminary stage. There was so much better to come. But that would have to wait. Ember set off back through the forest to her small make-shift shelter. As her home drew closer and closer, she could make out the figure of her mother standing, waiting. Her chestnut hair was now plagued with streaks of grey, and the dark circles under her eyes, coupled with her sagging shoulders, betrayed that she had not slept that night. Ember's heart fluttered with the painful realization that her mother wasn't strong anymore. In her hands she clutched the end piece of a moldy loaf of bread. Hanging from her body was the only clothing she had left, a coarse, tan tablecloth with places torn out for a head and two arms. In anticipation of her daughter's return, Ember's mother took a few steps forward, then thought better of it and retreated back the way she came. When Ember finally reached her, her mother tentatively held out the moldy piece of bread. Ember took it, scraped off the mold, and handed it back to her mother, declaring, "You need it more than I do".

"Ember, please, take it. You'll have better luck with the game tomorrow." Her mother had found her voice.

"I think we both know that there isn't any game left. We won't be able to eat, and I'd rather not draw out my death. This world? It's over." Ember's defiance was fierce, and deep inside she knew there was something worth living for, but she would never admit that to her mother. The love Ember had for her was stronger than anything, and the young girl was willing to do what she had to to help her mother survive.

"Do you know why your father and—"

"Don't speak of my father when you did nothing to try and save his life!" Ember's anger burst forth, she could not control herself. "Do you know how many countless nights I have lain in my bed and expected Daddy to come kiss me goodnight?! Do you know—"

Both of them froze. Something wasn't right. Their cabin shook on its weak foundations, and the ground beneath Ember's bare feet trembled. Mother and daughter shared a look of pure fear. Was this another attack? God knew what more the Pangaeans wanted. They had ripped all Ember held dear from her life. Fury tore through her heart; never had she hated anything more than the Pangaeans, with their filthy ways and darkened hearts. This time, she would not allow an attack. It just wasn't going to happen.

Ember lifted her head to the sky, searching for any sign of the bomber jets. Nothing. She had a clear view of the ocean; no naval armies were in sight. What was this trickery? As Ember's mind furiously swept through all the ways that the Pangaeans could attack, the dirt beneath her feet was growing warmer and warmer. In some places the ground was splitting apart, and molten lava was trickling out. Ember's mother's eyes grew wide as she watched the cracks growing wider and longer, and didn't find her voice until it was too late.

With a mighty roar, the ground beneath Ember's feet split open, lava poured out, and Ember just managed to stumble out of the way without any major burns. By now, the Earth was violently shaking; neither Ember nor her mother could walk two steps without falling to their hands and knees. Ember watched as her makeshift home collapsed, huge stones tumbled down, and helplessly, she watched as the limp form of her mother was crushed by the slab of granite they had used as a ceiling. A strangled cry burst forth from Ember's lips, for although she had never forgiven her for leaving Daddy and Sal to the soldiers, she was still her mother. Sobs racked her body as she remembered those last harsh words she had shared with her mother. And now she was dead. Gone, never to walk this Earth again.

Ember's survival instincts kicked in, and she leaped from fragment of ground to fragment of ground, avoiding piles of lava that seeped into every crevice they could find. The moment her feet touched solid ground, she put all she had into running, sprinting for her life. The next hours were a blur of pain and destruction. Everywhere she looked, Ember saw cracked, dry earth, and blackened tree stumps scattered across the land. Her heart felt empty; she was truly alone.

As the grey sunset faded, and the air grew cold, Ember stretched out her legs and inspected the burns that would undoubtedly invite infections. There was no longer skin on the soles of her feet. All that remained was a mass of mangled bloody flesh. The white tip of a bone peeked through, and she could already see the edges of the wound turning a sickly yellow-green. For the first time since the ground split, every inch of Ember's body screamed in pain. Bright bursts of color appeared before her eyes, and she found herself growing lightheaded and dizzy. As darkness eased in from the corners of her eyes, Ember found herself staring at small speck in the distance. Was it moving? Oh yes. Its pace was similar to that of a sloth or snail, but it was definitely moving. A dull ringing throbbed in Ember's ears, and her unconscious body slumped over. The speck crept closer. As it padded up to Ember's side, its dark golden eyes took in her inconvenient state of health.

Morning came all too soon for Ember. She ached all over, and she could tell that the infection in her foot was spreading.

Struggling to sit up, her fingers brushed something warm and coarse. Ember's eyes took a second to focus before she could make out the wild creature next to her. Her heart stopped. Lying in front of her, paws crossed, was a feral albino wolf. Quickly, she averted her eyes to avoid a challenge of the stronger animal's authority and strength. Ember sat frozen, her eyes locked on a small pebble, safely away from the wolf's gaze.

After hours of being completely still, Ember had cramps all over, and half of her body had fallen asleep. Suddenly, and without warning, the albino creature rose, and padded up to Ember. She became stiff with fear, and her heart was pounding. The wolf dipped its wet nose down and touched the side of Ember's face. And then it was gone. There was no puff of smoke, no otherworldly lights. It just disappeared. Shaking uncontrollably, Ember slowly turned her head; there was nothing in sight. Slightly relaxed, she began her search for two pointed stones. She would kill it before it killed her. She scoured all the land within one hundred feet, but found nothing. Ember was limp with defeat. Here, she would die, eaten alive by an albino wolf. Here, her bones would sink into the Earth, grey and carrying the scent of death.

A forlorn cry split the still air, it had returned. Pounding across the open plains at full speed, was the lone wolf. Ember's head snapped up, terror racing through her heart. She made a split decision, struggling to her feet and taking off running as fast as she could. She didn't get very far. With the first few stumbling steps, Ember's ankle made a distinct crunch, and she collapsed, wailing in pain. With trembling hands she pulled away the rough, brown breeches from her leg. Her ankle and foot were a mush of blood, pus, and what little flesh there was left. A yellow substance oozed out of the infection, slowly dripping onto the dirt. Ember squeezed shut her eyes, tilted her head back, and slowly rocked back and forth. *It's only a dream; it's only a dream* she told herself. But the hot breath down her neck told her otherwise.

This time, she accepted her fate. This loner could kill her now, and she couldn't care less. She no longer wanted to live. Ember turned to face the wolf; she looked into its eyes, inviting an attack. But the creature standing in front of her had kindness in its large golden eyes. In its mouth it held leafy things that could only be calendula flowers, and slightly wilted, but still green comfrey leaves. The beast dipped its head and deposited the food on the ground in front of Ember. Her mind was racing. *Has this wolf brought me food? Does it want me to survive?* The loner nudged the vegetation towards Ember, and she reached out to take a flower. She brought it to her mouth, reveling in the idea of eating. As soon as her lips touched the food, the wolf erupted in a series of loud, quick barks. Ember dropped it, stunned. She didn't understand. The albino creature had given her food. Did it want her to eat? But as soon as she made like she would obey him, he reprimanded her, barking harshly. And then it hit her. Back home after the war, she and her mother treated any burns or infections that passerbys had acquired with a mixed poultice of comfrey leaves and calendula flowers. The wolf was healing her. He did not intend for the food to go into her belly, but rather onto her wounds.

Ember crawled around gathering small twigs that would provide excellent kindling. Finding two sticks that were bigger and sturdier than the rest, she set about fiercely spinning them together, and soon a steady stream of ashy smoke was trailing upwards towards the bleak sky. It took time, but Ember soon coaxed a flame out of the dry sticks. She constructed a sort of spit, like the ones they use for meat. Ember placed the leaves and flowers vertically across two horizontal sticks. This way, when one side was finished cooking, she simply had to pick them up by the cool side, and flip them over. Her method worked, and soon she had a pile of warm greens. Laying the leaves and flowers on the ground, Ember mashed them together using the palms of her hands. The whole while she worked, the wolf sat watching. It never moved. With the fire still going strong, Ember carefully spread the poultice onto her infection, and let out a breath of relief as it quickly took effect. For the first time since the quakes, Ember felt strong. And she owed it all to the creature sitting across from her.

As night fell, the beast crept closer to the fire, its eyes glittering in the flames. The sparks flying everywhere gave it an otherworldly look. Ember realized that she owed her life to this animal. She felt protective of it, and wanted to give it a name. To make it feel loved. But this troubled her. Would naming the albino take away its power? By labeling this wolf forever, would she be taming his true spirit?

Ember thought about this. She realized naming something isn't taking away its power. It is quite the opposite. Not only did they give power, names were power. So Ember would give this albino creature a name true to his soul. She called him Sverre. In Old Norse, this meant 'wild'. And wild he was. Ember was confident in his masculinity, for he was bigger than most wolves, especially the females, and he carried an air about him that suggested he had once been the leader of his pack. She said his name out loud several times, liking the way it rolled off her tongue. Soon Ember grew weary and drifted off to sleep, content with her choice.

Dawn found girl and wolf side by side, sleeping soundly. The fire had reduced to small sparks, sputtering out in a matter of seconds. Sverre's white fur was dusty with specks of dirt, and his nose was dry and warm to the touch. His golden eyes eased open, dull and glazed over with pain. Sverre rose and padded a few feet away from Ember, his sides heaved as he struggled to choke something out. The painful-sounding noises coming from Sverre woke Ember, and she carefully stood, and limped over to him. By now, Sverre was having trouble breathing. Ember tentatively put her hand on his back. She got no reaction from the wolf, so she decided it was safe to continue. She eased into his view until she was crouched directly in front of him. He looked her in the eyes, and the fear reflected in them was undeniable. He told her this could be the end.

Ember lifted her head to the sky, looking for an answer. Sverre had saved her life, and now it was time for her to return the favor. Gently, she lifted his muzzle until she could look into his gaping jaws. There, lodged firmly in his throat, was a sharp bone.

Poor thing, thought Ember, *he must have accidentally swallowed it while eating his meal.* She took a deep breath, and holding his jaws securely so as they would not snap closed, Ember reached her hand to the back of his throat. Sverre began to growl, and Ember could tell that his gag reflex was going crazy. Her fingers struggled to catch hold of the slick bone, but once she had it, there was no letting go. She twisted it this way and that, trying not to scratch his sensitive throat. With a final tug, the bone came loose, and Ember triumphantly held it up for Sverre to see. The wolf crept closer to her, burying his head in her shoulder. Ember was careful as she wrapped her arms around his neck. She didn't squeeze him, and soon he slumped down, exhausted from his near-death experience.

Ember lay on her back, her eyes searching the clouds above. Was there any hope? A deep sadness crept into her heart, and she brought her hand to her face, wiping away the unwanted tears. Her arm brushed against something soft embedded in the ground. Curious, Ember sat up, examining the dusty floor of nature. There, creeping up from the ground was a small seedling. The tiny sprout was vibrantly green, with little leaves protruding from the slender stem. Ember's heart raced, what was happening? The cracked dirt around the plant gave no sign of containing water, and she wondered how the tiny bit of life survived. Ember decided to leave it alone, lest she harm it.

The days passed solemnly and without activity. The vegetables Sverre brought Ember each day had almost completely healed her wounds; and the wolf soon began to bring back meat. It was never much, but it kept them alive. Ember eventually grew sad. After all, what were the chances she would survive? She found a stick, and set about inscribing the dirt all around. Sometimes she drew things, but mostly she wrote. She wrote about the quakes, and Sverre. She wrote about her mother. She wrote about the Earth.

This Earth? She was once beautiful. This Earth? She once sang the glorious praises of life. There was no doubt in her mind that she would survive. Not anymore. Now she sits; a shadow. Wrapped in a fog of misery. The universe has had no mercy, she is a barren wasteland. The scent of death lingers on every blackened tree stump, every rotten blade of grass. Not a bird shares his song, not a creature stirs.

Time and time again, Ember thought of her mother. She thought of her father and Sal. She missed them. And time and time again, nothing changed. The wastelands remained.

There were no seasons anymore, so it was impossible to determine when it happened. But whenever it was, it changed Ember's life, forever. By the thousands, small sprouts popped up as far as Ember could see. They were everywhere. The dried up rivers slowly refilled, and small mice scampered through the grass, running from Sverre. Each night Ember would light a fire. Sverre would lay by her side and they would listen to the crickets, and gaze up at the stars. How beautiful they were.

**Eliza Sanders** has been writing since she picked up a pencil. She was born in Decatur, Georgia and is currently a sophomore at Decatur High. Eliza fell in love with horses at a young age, and has been riding at Little Creek for two years now. She lives with her parents, twin sister, two dogs, cat, and imaginary horse. One day, Eliza hopes to travel the world and learn as many languages as she can; but for now she's sticking with Spanish.

Critical Reading Questions and Writing Exercises

These critical reading questions and writing exercises are designed to enable young readers to engage with and explore the literature of the young writers of this anthology. Each question or exercise includes a reference to one or more of the Common Core State Standards with which it aligns. A listing of those standards is included at the end of this section for reference purposes.

"Not Alone"

1. The author uses a lot of powerful verbs, particularly with inanimate objects: shadows danced, the fog collected, etc. What is the effect of using verbs in this way?
[CCSS-ELA-Literacy.RL.9-10.4, 11-12.4]

2. Think of a time when the atmosphere or mood did not fit the setting, such as a normally happy place that was suddenly frightening. Write a piece in which you create an atmosphere that contrasts with the setting.
[CCSS-ELA-Literacy.W.9-10.3, 11-12.3]

"Reflections"

1. How does the author use the mirror to reveal information about the characters and their background? How is the mirror more effective than if the author told you that information in prose? List specific examples.
[CCSS-ELA-Literacy.RL.9-10.5, 11-12.5]

2. Think of an object and then think of a situation or setting where that object does not normally fit. Write a piece about a character's or characters' interaction with that object.
[CCSS-ELA-Literacy.W.9-10.3 11-12.3]

"Stormy"

    1. How does the narrator use nature to tell the story? Support your response with details from the text.
[CCSS-ELA-Literacy.RL.9-10.1, 11-12.1]

    2. Write a piece in which the main conflict is unknown. The characters react to it, but the reader does not know what it is for part or all of the story.
[CCSS-ELA-Literacy.W.9-10.4, 11-12.4]

"Instructions for Anxiety Attacks"

    1. Most fiction is written in first person point of view (I, me) or third person point of voice (he, she). Why do you think the author used second person (you)? What is the effect?
[CCSS-ELA-Literacy.RL.9-10.5, 11-12.5]

    2. Write a story in the second person in which you tell the reader to do something or go somewhere unusual.
[CCSS-ELA-Literacy.W.9-10.3, 11-12.3]

"The Doorman"

    1. The author uses very specific details. For example, rather than saying the doorman was tall, he is six feet five inches. He gets a beer on Wednesday nights. How do these specific details work or not work in the story? Give examples.
[CCSS-ELA-Literacy.RL.9-10.1, 11-12.1]

    2. Think of a person you've glimpsed only once or pass by every day but no nothing about. Write their story.
[CCSS-ELA-Literacy.W.9-10.3, 11-12.3]

"Mirror"

1. The poem contrasts reality with how the poet sees himself. What is the difference between the two?
[CCSS-ELA-Literacy.RL.9-10.2, 11-12.2]

2. What kind of person do you see when you look in the mirror? Is it the same kind of person others believe you to be? Perhaps you realize that your view of yourself deviates from the truth in some way. Write a piece in which you explore the difference between how you see yourself and another vision of you.
[CCSS-ELA-Literacy.W.9-10.2, 11-12.2]

"Suffer in Silence"

1. In this poem, several sets of lines are indented. What do these formatting shifts signal to the reader? Tip: the answer may not be the same for each set of lines.
[CCSS-ELA-Literacy.RL.9-10.5, 11-12.5]

2. Think of a short statement you have heard on at least one occasion. Why was that statement important and what do they reveal about situations that have developed since then. Write a piece in which you explore the impact it has on you today.
[CCSS-ELA-Literacy.W.9-10.2, 11-12.2]

"Please Answer"

1. How does the poet's formatting choices add dynamic depth to the event being portrayed in the poem?
[CCSS-ELA-Literacy.RL.9-10.5, 11-12.5]

2. Think of a situation in which sounds and voices might be heard over and around the events that are occurring. Write a poem or short story in which you incorporate those ancillary sounds in a meaningful manner.
[CCSS-ELA-Literacy.W.9-10.3, 11-12.3]

"Back When"

    1. What do the lines between teardrop 3 and 6 mean? Tip: the poet may have intentionally left that thought incomplete. What significance do these lines have in context?
[CCSS-ELA-Literacy.RL.9-10.5, 11-12.5]

    2. This poem counts tears as a way of measuring time. Write a piece that includes you counting something; it may be laughs or snores or anything that's relevant to a topic you wish to write about. Your counting should serve at least one clear function.
[CCSS-ELA-Literacy.W.9-10.4, 11-12.4]

"Mad Hatter"

    1. What has happened to Alice? Support your response with details from the poem.
[CCSS-ELA-Literacy.RL.9-10.3, 11-12.3]

    2. Your writing can benefit from incorporating or alluding to characters from famous works. Select a pair or trio of characters from a work that your readers would immediately recognize and remember. Then, write a piece that uses those characters to illustrate some aspect of a completely different situation.
[CCSS-ELA-Literacy.W.9-10.3, 11-12.3]

"The Last Words of this Poem are a Lie"

    1. Explain whether or not the title of this poem is true. Cite at least three specific details from the text of the poem in support of your position.
[CCSS-ELA-Literacy.RL.9-10.1, 11-12.1]

    2. Write down a statement. Now write a poem or short story that demonstrates that the statement you wrote down is not true.
[CCSS-ELA-Literacy.W.9-10.4, 11-12.4]

"Twelve Years of Holly Trees"

1. Explain four aspects of friendship the poet sees symbolized in a holly tree. Refer to specific lines from the poem in your response.
[CCSS-ELA-Literacy.RL.9-10.1, 11-12.1]

2. Write down an abstract concept such as friendship and then a type of plant. Write a poem that shows how aspects of the plant you chose symbolizes aspects of the concept.
[CCSS-ELA-Literacy.W.9-10.4, 11-12.4]

"Corporate Cannibals Churn Out Ghosts"

1. How do the images in the poem underscore and develop the contrasting images in the title of "corporate" and "cannibals?" Explain the meaning of at least two of the images.
[CCSS-ELA-Literacy.RL.9-10.2, 11-12.2]

2. Zombies have become quite popular. Write a poem or short story in which you use the concept of a zombie as a symbol of a social issue or problem.
[CCSS-ELA-Literacy.W.9-10.3, 11-12.3]

"Bastard Children"

1. Explain who you think the three children in the poem are. Refer to specific details in the poem to support your ideas and conclusions.
[CCSS-ELA-Literacy.RL.9-10.1, 11-12.1]

2. List out three people that you know. List out comparisons of their qualities. Write a poem or short essay that describes each person for your reader.
[CCSS-ELA-Literacy.W.9-10.2, 11-12.2]

"Fears"

1. Analyze the effect the repetition of the word "fear" has on the reader. How does it amplify the energy and force of the poem?
[CCSS-ELA-Literacy.RL.9-10.4, 11-12.4]

2. Choose an emotion you want to explore. Write a poem in which you use the technique of repetition to emphasize the qualities of that emotion for the reader.
[CCSS-ELA-Literacy.W.9-10.4, 11-12.4]

"Treasure"

1. How does this poem contrast two different types of treasure? What does it have to say about each types? Cite specific details from the text to support your answer.
[CCSS-ELA-Literacy.RL.9-10.2, 11-12.2]

2. Consider a concept that has two different perspectives. Write a short essay or poem that contrasts the two different perspectives and examines the topic from each viewpoint.
[CCSS-ELA-Literacy.W.9-10.2, 11-12.2]

"Redefined"

1. Analyze the manner in which the details of the setting enhances and reinforces the central meanings of the poem. Cite specific details from the text.
[CCSS-ELA-Literacy.RL.9-10.2, 11-12.2]

2. Think of a place or time. Write a poem or short story in which you emphasize details of the setting to communicate key ideas and concepts to the reader.
[CCSS-ELA-Literacy.W.9-10.4, 11-12.4]

"Born to Die"

1. Analyze what the use of quick snapshot-like images says about the nature of truth? Cite specific details from the text. [CCSS-ELA-Literacy.RL.9-10.1, 11-12.1]

2. Think about the concept of truth and the relationship of truth to perspective. Write a short essay, story or poem that explores how perspectives influence people's concept of truth. [CCSS-ELA-Literacy.W.9-10.2, 11-12.2]

"Blue's Clues"

1. How does this poem make use of allusion? What added dimensions does the reference to popular culture add to the poem? [CCSS-ELA-Literacy.RL.9-10.4, 11-12.4]

2. Think of a television show or movie you have seen. Write a poem, short story or essay that is inspired by and alludes to that television show or movie. [CCSS-ELA-Literacy.W.9-10.4, 11-12.4]

"Wasted"

1. What feelings does this poem attempt to recreate for the reader? How are those feelings central to the meaning of the poem? [CCSS-ELA-Literacy.RL.9-10.2, 11-12.2]

2. Write a poem or short story in which you attempt to capture an intense emotional or physical experience. Use descriptive language to help the reader enter into that experience. [CCSS-ELA-Literacy.W.9-10.3, 11-12.3]

"Banished"

1. Look at the several words and images that evoke the concept of time. What observations doe this poem make about the nature of time?
[CCSS-ELA-Literacy.RL.9-10.2, 11-12.2]

2. Compose a poem, short story or essay in which you explore an abstract concept such as time, love, anger, courage, etc. Use images and vocabulary that embody that concept.
[CCSS-ELA-Literacy.W.9-10.2, 11-12.2]

"Mindless Me"

1. What is this poem saying about the concept of mindlessness? Cite specific details from the text that support your answer.
[CCSS-ELA-Literacy.RL.9-10.1, 11-12.1]

2. Imagine a person who others would call mindless. Write a short character description that captures the qualities of that person and his or her mindless state.
[CCSS-ELA-Literacy.W.9-10.4, 11-12.4]

"The World"

1. How does the poems use of word play enhance the effect and meaning of the poem? Cite specific details from the poem to support your response.
[CCSS-ELA-Literacy.RL.9-10.4, 11-12.4]

2. Make a list of words that sound similar when you say them. They write a short poem in which you use those words in a playful manner.
[CCSS-ELA-Literacy.W.9-10.4, 11-12.4]

"Tea With my Town"

1. What emotion(s) is the author trying to convey or conceal through the participation of this gathering / social. What is the author's agenda for this event?
[CCSS-ELA-Literacy.RL.9-10.5, 11-12.5]

2. This style of writing indicates that there is teasing, taunting, and control. Write a poem or story that captures and expresses a feeling.
[CCSS-ELA-Literacy.W.9-10.3, 11-12.3]

"Antimony's Prayer"

1. What obstacles did the author have to overcome in this poem? Support your answer with details from the text of the poem.
[CCSS-ELA-Literacy.RL.9-10.1, 11-12.1]

2. Think of an obstacle you have had to overcome. Write a poem, story or short essay that describes what it took for you to overcome the obstacle.
[CCSS-ELA-Literacy.W.9-10.3, 11-12.3]

"The Instant After"

1. What are the images in this poem saying about moments in time? What is the narrator in the poem trying to capture?
[CCSS-ELA-Literacy.RL.9-10.2, 11-12.2]

2. Imagine your mind is like a camera. Look around you and take a mental snapshot of the moment you are in. Then write a poem, short story or essay that allows a reader to see that moment as you have seen it.
[CCSS-ELA-Literacy.W.9-10.4, 11-12.4]

"Unravel"

1. Describe the numerous ways in which the poem evokes the idea of music and sound. How do specific instances enhance the meaning of the poem?
[CCSS-ELA-Literacy.RL.9-10.2, 11-12.2]

2. Think of a sense other than sight (hearing, touch, taste, smell). Compose a poem or short story in which you emphasize that sense in the imagery and words you use.
[CCSS-ELA-Literacy.W.9-10.4, 11-12.4]

"Haste"

1. Describe the type of person this poem portrays. How would you imagine this person would be as a friend? Support your response with specific details from the text.
[CCSS-ELA-Literacy.RL.9-10.3, 11-12.3]

2. Write a poem that captures the essence of a person that you know. Show qualities of that person through his or her actions and attitudes..
[CCSS-ELA-Literacy.W.9-10.2, 11-12.2]

"The Day My Trampoline Died"

1. What is it that the trampoline symbolizes? How does the concept of a trampoline interact with the other images contained in the poem?
[CCSS-ELA-Literacy.RL.9-10.2, 11-12.2]

2. Think of a physical activity that you like to do. Compose a poem or short story in which that physical activity serves as an symbol or metaphor for your emotions or state of mind.
[CCSS-ELA-Literacy.W.9-10.4, 11-12.4]

"Don't Judge Me"

1. This poem is a series of short, fast lines. What is the effect of this structure? Cite specific details from the poem that support your answer.
[CCSS-ELA-Literacy.RL.9-10.5, 11-12.5]

2. Write a piece that uses mostly short, one-syllable words. Now rewrite the same piece using longer or multi-syllable words. What is the effect? How does the meaning or mood of the piece change with the word choice?
[CCSS-ELA-Literacy.W.9-10.4, 11-12.4]

"Father"

1. The last lines of the poem are "Sure you may be my father | But my daddy isn't you." What is the difference between a "father" and a "daddy" in this poem?
[CCSS-ELA-Literacy.RL.9-10.4, 11-12.4]

2. Write a piece about two family members facing a problem. Focus on how the relationship (good or bad) between the family members affect how they handle the problem.
[CCSS-ELA-Literacy.W.9-10.2, 11-12.2]

"Daughter"

1. How do the narrator's emotions change throughout the poem? Try reading the poem aloud. Do you notice any difference in how you say certain passages?
[CCSS-ELA-Literacy.RL.9-10.3, 11-12.3]

2. Create two characters. The first character chooses to stop being one type of person and becomes someone new. The second character is forced to stop being who they want to be due to something outside their control. Write a piece in which these two characters interact. Show the differences in their two stories.
[CCSS-ELA-Literacy.W.9-10.3, 11-12.3]

"What If?"

1. The poem imagines life as a video game. Find three specific examples of video game imagery and describe how they work to reveal the poem's meaning. Where does the poet move away from the game metaphor? Why?
[CCSS-ELA-Literacy.RL.9-10.5, 11-12.5]

2. Write a piece in which the fictional characters in your favorite game, book, or movie know they are fictional.
[CCSS-ELA-Literacy.W.9-10.3, 11-12.3]

"Misfit"

1. Look at the instances where the narrator mentions other people. How do they treat her? How does that make her respond? Why do you think she feels she has to respond in this way?
[CCSS-ELA-Literacy.RL.9-10.3, 11-12.3]

2. Write three versions of the same short poem. The first version has all rhyming lines, the second has some rhymes, and the third has no rhymes. Think about the changes in rhythm and word choice and how that affects the meaning of the poems.
[CCSS-ELA-Literacy.W.9-10.4, 11-12.4]

"Rebirth"

1. What is the significance of names in the story? Cite specific details from the text that support your response.
[CCSS-ELA-Literacy.RL.9-10.4, 11-12.4]

2. Think of a catastrophic event, anything from a zombie apocalypse to being caught in your underwear at prom. Describe what happens after.
[CCSS-ELA-Literacy.W.9-10.3, 11-12.3]

Common Core State Standards, Reading: Literature

CCSS.ELA-Literacy.RL.9-10.1
Cite strong and thorough textual evidence to support analysis of what the text says explicitly as well as inferences drawn from the text.

CCSS.ELA-Literacy.RL.9-10.2
Determine a theme or central idea of a text and analyze in detail its development over the course of the text, including how it emerges and is shaped and refined by specific details; provide an objective summary of the text.

CCSS.ELA-Literacy.RL.9-10.3
Analyze how complex characters develop over the course of a text, interact with other characters, and advance the plot or develop the theme.

CCSS.ELA-Literacy.RL.9-10.4 Determine the meaning of words and phrases as they are used in the text, including figurative and connotative meanings; analyze the cumulative impact of specific word choices on meaning and tone.

CCSS.ELA-Literacy.RL.9-10.5 Analyze how an author's choices concerning how to structure a text, order events within it create such effects as mystery, tension, or surprise.

CCSS.ELA-Literacy.RL.11-12.1 Cite strong and thorough textual evidence to support analysis of what the text says explicitly as well as inferences drawn from the text, including determining where the text leaves matters uncertain.

CCSS.ELA-Literacy.RL.11-12.2 Determine two or more themes or central ideas of a text and analyze their development over the course of the text, including how they interact and build on one another to produce a complex account; provide an objective summary of the text.

CCSS.ELA-Literacy.RL.11-12.3 Analyze the impact of the author's choices regarding how to develop and relate elements of a story or drama.

CCSS.ELA-Literacy.RL.11-12.4 Determine the meaning of words and phrases as they are used in the text, including figurative and connotative meanings; analyze the impact of specific word choices on meaning and tone, including words with multiple meanings or language that is particularly fresh, engaging, or beautiful.

CCSS.ELA-Literacy.RL.11-12.5 Analyze how an author's choices concerning how to structure specific parts of a text contribute to its overall structure and meaning as well as its aesthetic impact.

CCSS.ELA-Literacy.RL.11-12.6 Analyze a case in which grasping a point of view requires distinguishing what is directly stated in a text from what is really meant.

Common Core State Standards, Writing

CCSS.ELA-Literacy.W.9-10.2 Write informative/explanatory texts to examine and convey complex ideas, concepts, and information clearly and accurately through the effective selection, organization, and analysis of content.

CCSS.ELA-Literacy.W.9-10.3 Write narratives to develop real or imagined experiences or events using effective technique, well-chosen details, and well-structured event sequences.

CCSS.ELA-Literacy.W.9-10.4 Produce clear and coherent writing in which the development, organization, and style are appropriate to task, purpose, and audience.

CCSS.ELA-Literacy.W.11-12.2 Write informative/explanatory texts to examine and convey complex ideas, concepts, and information clearly and accurately through the effective selection, organization, and analysis of content.

CCSS.ELA-Literacy.W.11-12.3 Write narratives to develop real or imagined experiences or events using effective technique, well-chosen details, and well-structured event sequences.

CCSS.ELA-Literacy.W.11-12.4 Produce clear and coherent writing in which the development, organization, and style are appropriate to task, purpose, and audience.

National Governors Association Center for Best Practices, Council of Chief State School Officers. *Common Core State Standards English Language Arts*. National Governors Association Center for Best Practices, Council of Chief State School Officers, Washington D.C. 2010

Permissions

Empowering young writers to say, **"I am my scholarship!"**

Open call for submissions to the
Young Writers Anthology!

See your work in print!

Become a published writer!

**Earn royalites that can help
you pay for college!s**

VerbalEyze Press is accepting submissions from young adult writers,
ages 13 to 22, in any of the following genres:

- poetry
- short story
- songwriting
- playwriting
- graphic novel
- creative non-fiction

For submission details, visit
www.verbaleyze.org

VerbalEyze serves to foster, promote and support the development
and professional growth of emerging young writers.

Writers Cooperative

VerbalEyze is a nonprofit organization whose mission is to foster, promote and support the development and professional growth of emerging young writers.

The *Young Writers Anthology* is published as a service of VerbalEyze in furtherance of its goal to provide young writers with access to publishing opportunities that they otherwise would not have.

Fifty percent of the proceeds received from the sale of the *Young Writers Anthology* are paid to the authors in the form of scholarships to help them advance in their post-secondary education.

For more information about VerbalEyze and how you can become involved in its work with young writers, visit www.verbaleyze.org.